WORLD CUP
2018

THE TEAMS, THE STARS, THE STORIES

Abbeville Press Publishers
New York · London

A portion of this book's proceeds are donated to the **Hugo Bustamante AYSO Playership Fund**, a national scholarship program to help ensure that no child misses the chance to play AYSO Soccer. Donations to the fund cover the cost of registration and a uniform for a child in need.

Text by Illugi Jökulsson
Design and layout: Árni Torfason

For the English-language edition
Editor: Will Lach
Production manager: Louise Kurtz
Layout: Ada Rodriguez
Copy editor: Sharon Lucas

PHOTOGRAPHY CREDITS

Getty Images: p. 6 (Mondragón: Warren Little), 11 (Alex Livesey), 11 (Bernd Wende/ullstein bild), 16 (Popperfoto), 17 (Popperfoto), 17 (Michael Kunkel/Bongarts), 18 (Brian Bahr), 19 (Ian Walton), 19 (Ashley Allen), 25 (Robbie Jay Barratt—AMA), 25 (Chris Brunskill Ltd), 32 (Harry How), 37 (Vavá/Pelé: Keystone/Hulton Archive), 43 (Vavá/Pelé: Keystone/Hulton Archive), 45 (Allsport Hulton), 46 (Allsport Hulton), 47 (Allsport UK), 48 (Popperfoto), 51 (Bob Thomas), 52 (Bob Thomas), 53 (Bob Thomas), 54 (Bob Thomas), 55 (Phil Cole/Allsport), 56 (Claudio Villa Archive), 57 (Eddy Lemaistre/Corbis), 59 (Robert Cianflone), 59 (Ian MacNicol).

Shutterstock: p. 6–7 (Denis Zhitnik), 6 (Ronaldo: Christian Bertrand), 7 (Trophy:A. RICARDO), 7 (Neymar/Messi: Maxisport), 7 (Wolf: Caromai), 9 (Luzhniki Stadium: Viacheslav Lopatin), 9 (Rungrado stadium: Viktoria Gaman), 10 (Russian fans: Marco Iacobucci EPP), 10 (Yashin: artnana), 12 (Buffon: Oleh Dubyna), 13 (Klose: AGIF), 14 (Suárez: AGIF), 14 (Cavani: Cosminlftode), 14 (Lewandowski: daykung), 15 (Agüero: CP DC Press), 15 (Salah: Alizada Studios), 15 (Azmoun: Marco Iacobucci EEP), 20 (CP DC Press), 22 (CP DC Press), 23 (Marco Iacobucci EPP), 24 (CP DC Press), 26 (Mitch Gunn), 27 (Dmytre Larin), 28 (CP DC Press), 29 (CP DC Press), 29 (Marco Iacobucci EPP), 30 (Cosminlftode), 31 (Laszlo Szirtesi), 34–35 (Cosminlftode), 35 (Marco Iacobucci EPP), 36 (Ververidis Vasilis), 58 (Oleh Dubyna).

Wikimedia Commons: p. 38, 39, 40, 41, 42, 43, 44, 45, 57

Árni Torfason: p. 17

First published in the United States of America in 2017 by Abbeville Press, 116 West 23rd Street, New York NY 10011

First Edition
10 9 8 7 6 5 4 3 2 1

ISBN 978-0-7892-1302-0

Library of Congress Cataloguing-in-Publication Data available upon request.

For bulk and premium sales and for text adoption procedures, write to Customer Service Manager, Abbeville Press, 116 West 23rd Street, New York, NY 10011, or call 1-800-ARTBOOK.

Visit Abbeville Press online at www.abbeville.com.

CONTENTS

A RUSSIAN TOURNAM

Cristiano Ronaldo plays at La Liga match between Valencia CF and Real Madrid at Mestalla on February 22, 2017, in Valencia, Spain.

On June 14, 2018, the Russians and Saudis will face each other in the Luzhniki Stadium in Moscow. This game will launch the most spectacular and popular sports event in the world: the FIFA World Cup, this time held in Russia. The eyes of soccer fans around the world will be trained on Russia for a month until the final takes place, on July 15, once again in the glorious Luzhniki Stadium, in the presence of 81,000 impassioned soccer fans. No one knows who will enter the field on that day. Will it be one of the famous soccer players that have now become household names? Will the magician Messi lead Argentina to victory? Will the goal-scoring genius Ronaldo lift the cup with his Portuguese comrades? Is it once again time for the yellow-clad Brazilian legends to reclaim the title, with the trickster Neymar in the lead? Or will a dark horse spring into the final and rise up as an unexpected victor? Despite the US's absence this year, there is no doubt that million of Americans will sit glued to their TV screens at the commencement of this dazzling and legendary soccer festival!

Aerial view of Stadium Luzhniki, Moscow, Russia.

The World Cup Trophy that every footballer dreams of lifting.

ENT

Zabivaka the wolf, the official mascot of the 2018 FIFA World Cup, at Moscow's Manezhnaya Square.

Leo Messi and Neymar of FC Barcelona celebrating during a Spanish League match against RCD Espanyol at the Power8 Stadium on April 25, 2015, in Barcelona, Spain.

THE VENUES

SAINT PETERSBURG

KALININGRAD

MOSCOW

NIZHNY NOVGOROD

SARANSK KAZAN YEKATERINBURG

SAMARA

VOLGOGRAD

ROSTOV-ON-DON

SOCHI

The first qualification game for the 2018 World Cup was played at the 13,000-capacity National Stadium at Dili, East Timor, on March 12, 2015. The East Timor forward Quito scored the first goal against Mongolia in the fourth minute. Despite the fact that neither East Timor (ranked 196th in the world) nor Mongolia (199th) managed to qualify for the final tournament in Russia, the level of passion in the Dili stadium was no less than that which will engulf the 11 magnificent venues that will serve as home to the tournament in the summer of 2018.

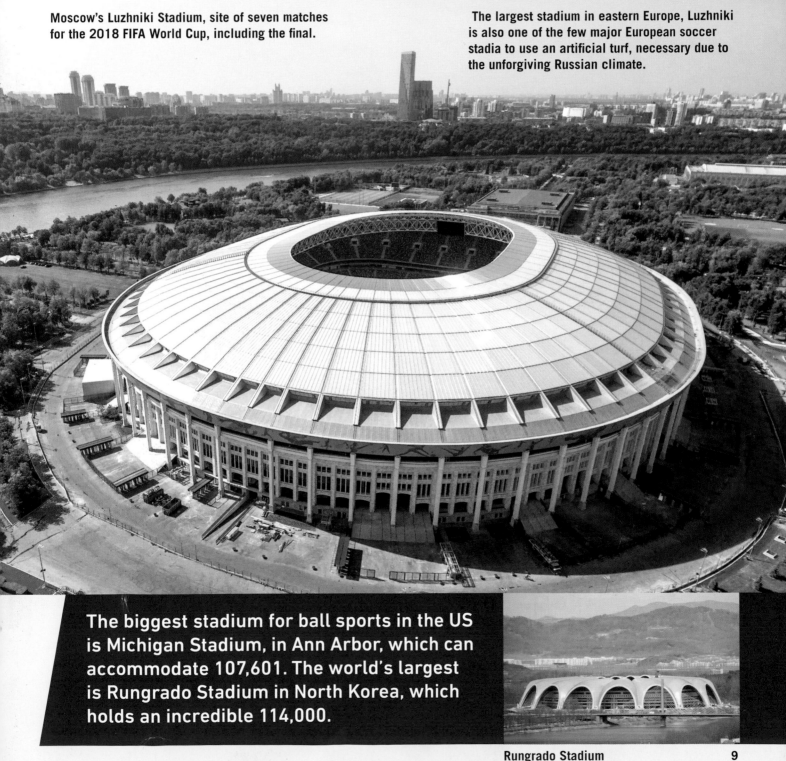

Moscow's Luzhniki Stadium, site of seven matches for the 2018 FIFA World Cup, including the final.

The largest stadium in eastern Europe, Luzhniki is also one of the few major European soccer stadia to use an artificial turf, necessary due to the unforgiving Russian climate.

The biggest stadium for ball sports in the US is Michigan Stadium, in Ann Arbor, which can accommodate 107,601. The world's largest is Rungrado Stadium in North Korea, which holds an incredible 114,000.

Rungrado Stadium

THE RUSSIAN TEAM

In order to enter the 2018 tournament, the Russian hosts were safe from competitive international games, and admittedly, their performances in recent friendlies have been rather less than impressive. However, maybe the Russian team will be filled with sudden inspiration when they face the Saudis on June 16, surrounded by 80,000 cheering spectators, including Vladimir Putin in person! Most of the players are bound to their home league in Russia, and are therefore mostly unknown to international audiences. Goalkeeper and captain Igor Akinfeev is a worthy candidate as heir to the Russian goalkeeping legacy—a long line of players who have dazzled the soccer world since the days of Yashin. And wise opponents should also beware of the

calculating midfielder Alan Dzagoev, and his companion, the sharpshooting forward Aleksandr Kokorin.

LEGENDS OF RUSSIAN SOCCER

Lev Yashin with Golden Ball, 1964.

Russians have always possessed a great soccer team. Under the name of the Soviet Union, the national team won the 1960 European Championships, and were the runners-up in 1964, 1972, and 1988. Their best World Cup achievement was landing fourth place in 1966. Russia's top player during that time was the legendary goalkeeper Lev Yashin, nicknamed the "Black Spider." Many considered him to have been the greatest goalkeeper in soccer history. What is more, a Russian player holds one of the most remarkable records in World Cup history. During the 1994 World Cup in the USA, Oleg Salenko scored an amazing five goals in Russia's 6–1 annihilation of the Cameroon national team.

WORLD CUP RECORDS

MOST SUCCESSFUL:

1. BRAZIL
2. GERMANY*
3. ITALY
4. ARGENTINA
5. SPAIN
6. ENGLAND
7. FRANCE
8. URUGUAY

*INCLUDING WEST GERMANY'S
PERFORMANCE 1954–1990.

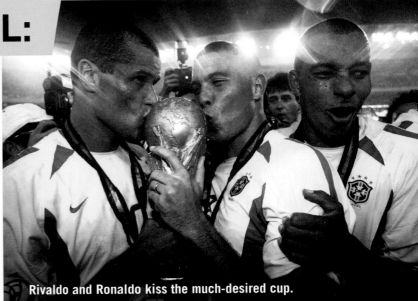

Rivaldo and Ronaldo kiss the much-desired cup.

WORLD CUP PARTICIPATION:

1.	BRAZIL	20*
2.	GERMANY	18**
3.	ITALY	18
4.	ARGENTINA	16
5.	SPAIN	14
6.	ENGLAND	14
7.	FRANCE	14
8.	URUGUAY	12

*BRAZIL HAS PARTICIPATED SINCE
THE START.
**INCLUDING WEST GERMANY'S
PARTICIPATION 1954–1990.

Lothar Matthäus often had cause to
celebrate during World Cup tournaments.

BIGGEST AUDIENCE:

1.	BRAZIL – URUGUAY 1950	171,772
2.	ARGENTINA – WEST GERMANY 1986	114,600
3.	BRAZIL – ITALY 1970	108,192

Estadio Centenario, in Montevideo, Uruguay, was the venue for the first World Cup in 1930.

MOST GAMES PLAYED IN THE WORLD CUP:

1.	LOTHAR MATTHÄUS, GERMANY	25	(1982–1998)
2.	MIROSLAV KLOSE, GERMANY	24	(2002–2014)
3.	PAOLO MALDINI	23	(1990–2002)
4.	DIEGO MARADONA	21	(1982–1994)
5.	UWE SEELER, WEST GERMANY	21	(1958–1970)

PLAYER PARTICIPATION:

Gianluigi Buffon

Lothar Matthäus played in five World Cup tournaments, first for West Germany and then Germany. The Mexican goalkeeper Antonio Carbajal also played in five tournaments, 1950–1966, but only played 11 games. Gianluigi Buffon has been selected to participate with the Italian team five times, 1998–2014, but did not play a game in the 1998 tournament.

MOST GOALS IN ONE GAME—AND THE OLDEST GOALSCORER:

Oleg Salenko scored five goals in Russia's 6–1 victory over Cameroon during the 1994 World Cup. In the same game, Roger Milla from Cameroon became the oldest goalscorer. He was 42 years old when he scored Cameroon's only goal.

OLDEST PLAYER:

The Colombian goalkeeper Faryd Mondragón was 43 when he came on as substitute in the game against Japan during the 2014 World Cup.

Faryd Mondragón

YOUNGEST PLAYER:

Norman Whiteside was 17 when he played for Northern Ireland against Yugoslavia in the 1982 World Cup.

HIGHEST NUMBER OF GOALS:

1. **KLOSE, GERMANY** — 16 GOALS IN 24 GAMES
2. **RONALDO, BRAZIL** — 15 GOALS IN 19 GAMES
3. **MÜLLER, WEST GERMANY** — 14 GOALS IN 13 GAMES
4. **FONTAINE, FRANCE** — 13 GOALS IN 6 GAMES
5. **PELÉ, BRAZIL** — 12 GOALS IN 14 GAMES
6. **KOCSIS, HUNGARY** — 11 GOALS IN 5 GAMES
7. **KLINSMANN, GERMANY*** — 11 GOALS IN 17 GAMES

*Including performances for West Germany in 1990

Klose

ALL-STAR GOALSCORERS

Luis Suárez celebrates a goal against England in Group D of the 2014 World Cup.

LUIS SUÁREZ
URUGUAY

Born 1987, Height: 6', Barcelona player.
International games: 95, Goals: 49

Suárez is one the world's most dangerous forwards when he is at his best. He can do it all: burst through defense, create goalscoring opportunities, and shoot. He ended 2010 with a red card for handball, and was suspended from the 2014 World Cup for biting an opponent. We will wait to see what will happen in Russia!

EDINSON CAVANI
URUGUAY

Born: 1987, Height: 6'½", PSG player.
International games: 96, Goals: 39

Edinson Cavani

One of the world's fiercest penalty-box predators—a master of stalking the area, receiving passes, then scoring. The Uruguayan team can reach far with him and Suárez in their best form.

ROBERT LEWANDOWSKI
POLAND

Born 1988, Height: 6'1"
Bayern München player.
International games: 91 Goals: 51

This incredible goalscorer has brought Poland far. He is most famous for scoring five beautiful goals for Bayern within nine minutes in September 2016.

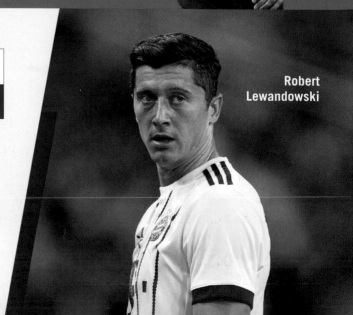
Robert Lewandowski

JAMES RODRIGUEZ
COLOMBIA
Born 1991, Height: 5'11"
Bayern München player.
International games: 59, Goals: 21

James Rodriguez

This sophisticated and strong attacking midfielder blossomed during the 2014 World Cup. He was the top scorer, with six goals, and played notably well. He has everything it takes to at least repeat this performance.

Sergio Agüero

SERGIO AGÜERO
ARGENTINA
Born 1988, Height: 5'8"
Manchester City player.
International games: 82, Goals: 33

Agüero is the world's toughest goalscorer—quick as a whip, with great balance, elegant shots, and total concentration. Agüero suffered an injury at the 2014 World Cup which might have lost Argentina the title. Agüero and Ángel Di María must both support Messi if the team is to stand a chance in Russia.

MOHAMED SALAH
EGYPT
Born 1992, Height: 5'9", Liverpool player.
International games: 56, Goals: 32

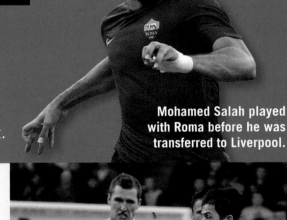

After a long wait, Egypt finally qualified for the World Cup. Egypt's passion is vast and the team might go far, if the lightning-quick and agile Salad is allowed to shine. His comrade at Liverpool, the Senegalese Sadio Mané, is expected to perform with great success in the tournament.

Mohamed Salah played with Roma before he was transferred to Liverpool.

SARDAR AZMOUN
IRAN
Born 1995, Height: 6'1"
Rubin Kazan player.
International games: 28, Goals: 22

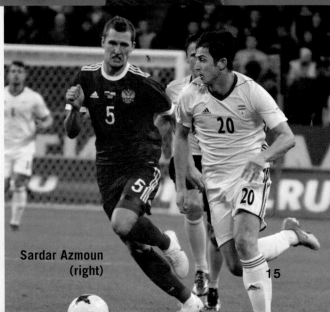

The strength of the Iranian team is unlikely to be great enough to make Azmoun the top goalscorer. However, he is extremely powerful, can score any type of goal, and here he represents the numerous players from the "weaker" soccer nations, who travel to Russia in order to realize their wildest hopes and dreams.

Sardar Azmoun (right)

THE US AT THE WORLD CUP

1930

The US participated in the first World Cup tournament in Uruguay. The national team played an amazing game in the group stages and defeated both Belgium and Paraguay 3–0. In the latter game, Bert Patenaude, from Fall River in Massachusetts, scored the first hat trick in World Cup history. This achievement was enough to secure a place for the US in the semifinals for the first and only time, where it was ultimately crushed by the powerful Argentine team.

1934

The US were defeated by Italy in their only game of the tournament. Italy went on to become the world champion.

1950

Not much was expected from the US team at this tournament. The team failed to advance from the group stages but it nevertheless achieved one great victory, perhaps one of the most unexpected in World Cup history. England was generally considered to be strongest soccer power in the world, but the US managed to defeat them 1-0. Many people who read about the victory in the newspaper refused to believe the results, and insisted that someone had made a typo, and the true score had been 10–1 in favor of England. It was the Haitian Joe Gaetjens who scored the winning goal, and the St. Louis goalkeeper Frank Borghil performed heroically, making key saves throughout the game.

Sadly, Joe Gaetjens (right) was killed during a coup in Haiti in 1964.

1990

After a 40-year break, the US finally made it back to the World Cup, this time held in Italy. The revitalization of soccer had just kicked off in the States, and the team lost all three games in the group stages.

1994

The US home team showed great signs of progress, and came third in their group, gaining them entry into the knockout phase. The US held Switzerland to a draw and then defeated the much-fancied Colombian team, but eventually lost to Romania. In the round of 16, the US team lost 0–1 to the eventual Brazilian world champions, which was considered a flattering result. The US team was composed of several legends, such as goalkeeper Tony Meola, defender Alexi Lalas, midfielder Cobi Jones, and the forward Eric Wynalda.

1998

The US once again returned to the final tournament, this time hosted by the French. Unfortunately the team failed to return to its 1994 form, and lost all three games.

2002

The World Cup tournament, held in Japan and South Korea, saw one of the US national team's best performances. Led by Bruce Arena, the dynamic team reached second place in the group stages, famously defeating the highly impressive Portuguese team, which included

Bert Patenaude scored a total of four goals in the 1930 tournament.

one of the world's greatest soccer players, Luis Figo. Brad Friedel vigilantly guarded the US goal, emboldening the midfield ranks, where the captain Claudio Reyna reigned supreme. The frontlines were manned by forwards Brian McBride and the young Landon Donovan. In the round of 16, the US team won a sweet victory over its perennial enemy, Mexico. The team then lost 0–1 to Germany in the quarterfinals.

Alexi Lalas and the 1994 team.

2006

In light of the US's impressive 2002 achievements, 2006 was a disappointment. In the group stages, a 1–1 draw with Italy was the only point scored, and the team was eliminated from the tournament.

2010

At the South African World Cup, the US came top in their group for the very first time. Tim Howard served as goalkeeper for a team captained by Carlos Bocanegra. Coach Bob Bradley positioned Clint Dempsey at the side of Landon Donovan at the front. In the first game, the team drew 1-1 with England. A draw with Slovenia and a hard-won victory over Algeria catapulted the US team to the round of 16, where they suffered defeat at the hands of the spirited Ghana in extra time.

2014

The US expected great things from the team sent to the World Cup in Brazil. Managed by Jürgen Klinsmann, the team progressed relatively comfortably from the group stages by defeating Ghana, drawing against mighty Portugal (captained by Cristiano Ronaldo), and then lost by a 0–1 whisker against eventual winners Germany. Many fans envisaged further success, but in the round of 16, the US was knocked out 1–2 in extra time by the super-strong Belgian team, which included the excellent Hazard, De Bruyne, and Lukaku.

Landon Donovan after a win against Mexico in the 2002 Cup.

2018

In what *Sports Illustrated* writer Grant Wahl called "the most surreal and embarrassing night in US soccer history," the US was eliminated from competition after losing 2–1 to Trinidad and Tobago, despite beating them 6–0 earlier in qualification. It is the first time since 1986 that the US will not play in a World Cup.

Clint Dempsey with English captain Steven Gerrard on him at the 2010 Cup.

Christian Pulisic after the loss to Trinidad and Tobago on October 10, 2017.

THE STARS AN

NEYMAR
FULL NAME:
NEYMAR DA SILVA SANTOS JÚNIOR
BORN: FEBRUARY 5, 1992
HEIGHT: 5'9"
TEAMS: SANTOS (BRAZIL),
BARCELONA (SPAIN), PSG (FRANCE)
INTERNATIONAL GAMES: 81
GOALS: 52

NEYMAR

BRAZIL

Neymar in a game against Uruguay.

Neymar is one of those soccer players who is always a pleasure to watch. He is energetic and agile, extremely quick, accurate in both passes and shots, and plays with everything he has. Neymar can sometimes come across as being arrogant on the field, and he left Barcelona so he wouldn't have to live in Messi's shadow, but he always brings life to the game, and his joy when playing is unquestionable. In Brazil it is common to refer to promising players as the "new Pelé," and when it comes to Neymar, the comparison is not so farfetched. Both are equally nimble and cunning with the ball, and though Neymar is not as powerful as Pelé, he is faster. In order to become a true equal to Pelé, Neymar will have to put every effort into winning the World Cup title in Russia, given the failure to do so as the home team in Brazil. One thing is for certain: Neymar will keep things lively!

D THE TEAMS

WILL NEYMAR LEAD BRAZIL TO VICTORY?

The last time Brazil won the world championship title was in 2002. The nation was bitterly disappointed by the performance of the home team at the 2014 World Cup in Brazil. Following Neymar's injury in the game against Colombia, the team was eliminated by way of a humiliating 7–1 defeat at the hands of the Germans. The national team appeared unconvincing and cumbersome a few years afterwards, too. Now, however, coach Tite is in the final stages of assembling a powerful team which should definitely deliver the dynamic samba-soccer that Brazil knows and loves.

Neymar is the major player on the team, but the lightning-quick Gabriel Jesus (born 1997, plays with Man. City) has relieved Neymar of some of the goal-scoring pressure. Who knows, perhaps the Brazilian national team will be adding the sixth star to their jersey after the 2018 World Cup in Russia!

Neymar is gaining the lead on Cristiano Ronaldo as the world's next best player. Interestingly, they are both born on the same day: February 5.

LIONEL "LEO" MESSI
FULL NAME: LIONEL ANDRÉS MESSI
BORN: JUNE 24, 1987
HEIGHT: 5'6"
TEAM: BARCELONA (SPAIN)
INTERNATIONAL GAMES: 123
GOALS: 61

MESSI

Messi during the 2014 World Cup in a Group F game against Iran.

Leo Messi has only two competitors to the title "greatest soccer player of history"—Pelé and Maradona. Messi has scored hundreds of beautiful goals and holds a host of records, but he is also always creating something for others, setting up goals for his teammates, and exciting fans of the game with his skill and cunning. And Messi has these traits in more abundance than his archenemy Cristiano Ronaldo. The Portuguese player is quick and agile, and a great athlete, but he is lacking Messi's artistic flair. Messi desires nothing more than to follow in the footsteps of his countryman Maradona,

and deliver the World Cup to Argentina. In the 2014 World Cup in Brazil, Messi managed to carry a dull team to the finals, but failed to lead them to victory. Messi will make every effort to ensure the world-champion title in Russia, but the question remains as to whether the rest of his teammates will join the effort. Argentina barely qualified, and now it remains to be seen whether Messi still has enough forward-thrust to his magical powers. And if Messi manages to win the title, the name of the world's greatest soccer player will be in no doubt whatsoever!

ISCO

FULL NAME: FRANCISCO ROMÁN ALARCÓN SUÁREZ
BORN: APRIL 21, 1992
HEIGHT: 5'10"
TEAMS: VALENCIA, MALAGA, REAL MADRID (ALL SPAIN)
INTERNATIONAL GAMES: 24
GOALS: 7

SPAIN

Isco is Spain's brightest star.

A few players remain from the legendary Spanish team that won three international tournaments 2008–2012, such as Sergio Busquets, Andrés Iniesta, and the captain Sergio Ramos. However, Spain's hopes for the 2018 World Cup must now be placed in new leaders, such as Isco. This highly skillful attacking midfielder has already become a star with Real Madrid. He can pick out extremely accurate passes, and he can dribble past anyone. Isco is also strong, creative, and a confident shot. Together with forward Álvaro Morata (now with Chelsea) and perhaps the old lion Diego Costa, Isco can perhaps reignite Spain's fighting spirit.

POGBA

FULL NAME: PAUL LABILE POGBA
BORN: MARCH 15, 1993
HEIGHT: 6'3"
TEAMS: JUVENTUS (ITALY), MANCHESTER UNITED (ENGLAND)
GAMES: 49
GOALS: 8

Pogba during the 2014 World Cup in a game against Ecuador.

POGBA

Sir Alex Ferguson has a special knack for discovering brilliant players, but he was mistaken with Paul Pogba. In his teens, the young Frenchman joined Manchester United but Ferguson paid no attention to him, so Pogba transferred to Juventus. There he was allowed to develop and played a part in injecting life back into Juventus following a number of meager years for the team. United was then forced to fork out a large sum to reclaim Pogba after the Euro in France. Pogba is still young and has yet to fully mature as a player, but at his current best he rolls like an unstoppable tank in midfield, then bursts forth, sets the offense into motion, and lunges toward the goal. With N'Golo Kanté behind him, in charge of the defense, Pogba acquires enough space to structure the offense and scare the living daylights out of his opponents with his relentless fighting-spirit.

CAN THE FRENCH MAKE UP FOR 2016?

After some great victories in Iceland and then in Germany during the 2016 Euro, it seemed like the French team was set to easily overpower the Portuguese team, especially given that Ronaldo left the field early in the game due to an injury. It turned out quite differently: home-team France lost 0–1 and the nation was in tears. The French team is now determined to make up for that loss by conquering Russia, and certainly has the right players for the job. The frontline is manned by Olivier Giroud (born 1986, Arsenal) as well as Atoine Griezmann (born 1991, Atlético Madrid). The young

Kingsley Coman (born 1996, Bayern Munich) is likely to set the field alight at any moment. In the defense there are Raphael Varane (born 1993, Real Madrid) and Samuel Umtiti (born 1993, Barcelona) whose day job is to keep their opponents in Spain in check. The towering Tottenham goalkeeper Hugo Lloris (born 1986) will be there, ready to receive the shots. Didier Deschamps still serves as the coach of the French national team. He was captain of the 1998 world-champion team, and wants nothing more than to clasp the cup once more!

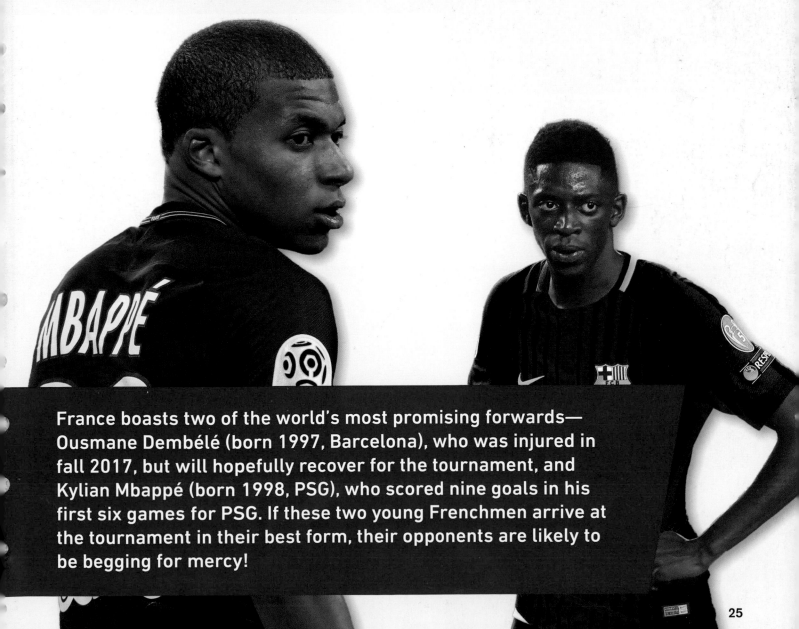

France boasts two of the world's most promising forwards— Ousmane Dembélé (born 1997, Barcelona), who was injured in fall 2017, but will hopefully recover for the tournament, and Kylian Mbappé (born 1998, PSG), who scored nine goals in his first six games for PSG. If these two young Frenchmen arrive at the tournament in their best form, their opponents are likely to be begging for mercy!

WILL GERMANY DEFEND THE TITLE?

Only twice in World Cup history has a team succeeded in defending their title (Italy in 1938 and Brazil in 1962). Don't be surprised if the Germans manage this feat in Russia 2018—they entered the 2014 World Cup with a young team, and most of the players are still in their best form. It is especially important that the midfield machine Toni Kroos (born 1990, Real Madrid) performs at the top of his game. Coach Joachim Löw has a number of great players to choose from, and in the 2017 FIFA Confederations Cup he presented a "reserve team" which conquered the tournament with ease. Many in that team have now developed into powerful players, such as defender Joshua Kimmich (Bayern), midfielders Leroy Sané (Man. City) and Leon Goretzka (Schalke), and the forward Timo Werner (Leipzig). The Germans will definitely put up a good fight in Russia!

MÜLLER
FULL NAME: THOMAS MÜLLER
BORN: SEPTEMBER 13, 1989
HEIGHT: 6'1"
TEAM: BAYERN MÜNCHEN (GERMANY)
INTERNATIONAL GAMES: 89
GOALS: 37

The forward Müller was close to unknown outside Germany when he appeared in the country's national team at the 2010 World Cup, at 20 years old. He scored five goals. He repeated the act in 2014 with another set of five. There is a good chance that Müller will play in both the 2018 and 2022 World Cups, and he could reach the upper echelon of the world's top goalscorers. Müller is tall, powerful, selfless, and diligent. He has an uncanny ability to find the areas in the opponent's defense where he can cause the most disruption, creating opportunities for teammates, or sneaking a shot himself.

MÜLLER

GERMANY

Müller celebrates in a game against Chelsea during the final of the 2012 FIFA Confederations Cup.

NEUER
FULL NAME: MANUEL PETER NEUER
BORN: MARCH 27, 1986
HEIGHT: 6'4"
TEAMS: SCHALKE, BAYERN MÜNCHEN (BOTH GERMANY)
INTERNATIONAL GAMES: 74
GOALS: 0

GERMANY

NEUER

Many great goalkeepers have played for Germany through the years, such as Sepp Maier (1974 World Cup), Oliver Kahn, and Jens Lehmann. Neuer is maybe the greatest of them all. The confidence that emanated from Neuer at the 2014 World Cup played no small part in Germany's triumph. Despite his height and bulk, he is remarkably quick and agile, and is renowned for leaving his goal to participate in building his team's offense.

Manuel Neuer in a match against Holland during the 2012 UEFA Euro.

HOW FAR WILL BELGIUM REACH?

Belgium has stealthily built a hugely powerful team, which casts a massive shadow on its neighbors in Holland, whose team failed to qualify for the World Cup. The Belgian team had a great start at the 2014 World Cup, but got eliminated by Argentina in the quarterfinals. Now many believe that the team can reach even further. There are great players on the team. One of the world's best goalkeepers, Thibaut Courtois (Chelsea), is a Belgian. Well-known players from the English league are in the defense, such as Vincent Kompany (Man. City), and Toby Alderweireld and Jan Vertonghen (both Tottenham). The controversial Marouane Fellaini (Man. United) mans the midfield. The Spaniard Roberto Martinez serves as coach, and he utilizes the attacking style that comes so naturally to the Belgians.

BELGIUM

HAZARD
FULL NAME:
EDEN MICHAEL HAZARD
BORN: JANUARY 7, 1991
HEIGHT: 5'8"
TEAMS: LILLE (FRANCE),
CHELSEA (ENGLAND)
INTERNATIONAL GAMES: 80
GOALS: 20

Hazard in World Cup 2014 in a match against Russia.

Eden Hazard is often compared to Leo Messi, and they have much in common. Both are short, extremely skillful, and both can breezily dribble through the opponent's defense to strike a gorgeous shot or deliver an elegant pass. On a good day, Hazard almost equals the Argentine genius!

WILL THE YOUNGER BROTHERS JOIN?
It is interesting to note that the younger brothers of both Hazard and Lukakus are now playing side-to-side with their older brothers on the national team and both stand a chance of joining the starting lineup. Jordan Lukaku (born 1994) is a strong left back with Lazio in Italy. He has played seven international games. The forward Thorgan Hazard (born 1993) plays with Borussia in Germany and he has already scored two goals in six international games.

DE BRUYNE
FULL NAME: KEVIN DE BRUYNE
BORN: JUNE 28, 1991
HEIGHT: 5'11"
TEAMS: GENK (BELGIUM), CHELSEA (ENGLAND), BREMEN, WOLFSBURG (BOTH GERMANY), MAN. CITY (ENGLAND)
INTERNATIONAL GAMES: 53
GOALS: 12

BELGIUM

De Bruyne in a match against Algeria at the 2014 World Cup.

DE BRUYNE

De Bruyne will turn 27 during the World Cup in Russia—the age when soccer players are at the top of their game. De Bruyne has incredible skills—he is an intelligent player, a lucid playmaker, and equally gifted with both shots and passes. It is close to unfair that one team boasts two such talented attacking midfielders, in the form of De Bruyne and Hazard. De Bruyne took his time to develop as a player, and when he played with Chelsea, coach José Mourinho seemed unsure of how to best harness his talent. After a stint with German teams, De Bruyne returned to England. Guardiola, coach of Man. City, made him playmaker in a great offensive team, and there the Belgian has flourished.

LUKAKU
FULL NAME: ROMELU LUKAKU
BORN: MAY 13, 1993
HEIGHT: 6'3"
TEAMS: ANDERLECHT (BELGIUM), CHELSEA, WBA, EVERTON, **MAN. UNITED (ALL ENGLAND)**
INTERNATIONAL GAMES: 61
GOALS: 25

BELGIUM

A tall and powerful forward who can break through almost any defense, Lukaku had a tough time at Chelsea when he started, but he properly came into his own with Everton. In fall 2017, Lukaku made a record with his new team Manchester United when he scored 10 goals in his first nine games. Lukaku is always a threat on the field but he sometimes needs help from friends. And Hazard and De Bruyne are perfect for the job, firing inch-perfect passes his way.

LUKAKU

Lukaku in a match against Italy during the 2016 Euro.

HARRY KANE
FULL NAME: HARRY EDWARD KANE
BORN: JULY 28, 1993
HEIGHT: 6'2"
TEAM: TOTTENHAM HOTSPUR (ENGLAND)
INTERNATIONAL GAMES: 23
GOALS: 12

It's invariably the same old story with England at the World Cup. The team breezes out of the group stages, but then suffers elimination when faced with a fierce opponent. In fact, England landed at the bottom of their group at the 2014 World Cup, which came as quite the shock. For the coming Russian challenge, the English have put their faith into a few Tottenham players, such as attacking midfielder Dele Alli and midfielders Eric Dier and Harry Winks, and particularly, Harry Kane. Kane was no boy prodigy—he was a late bloomer, and many pundits were unsure that he would make it to the top. However, he now counts among the world's greatest forwards. Kane is an all-round player, scores with both feet and his head, cleverly positions himself in the penalty area, where he has snuck in numerous goals, but he can also dribble and shoot from long distances. Most of all, he is sensible, down-to-earth, and has great composure. Manchester City player Raheem Sterling will join the Tottenham players for England, as well as Liverpool player Adam Lallana—both look set for grand achievements at the 2018 World Cup. However, the performances of the "Three Lions" will depend most of all on Harry Kane—and he has exactly what it takes to rack up the goals!

KANE

Harry Kane celebrates in a Champions League game against Borussia Dortmund.

CRISTIANO RONALDO
FULL NAME: CRISTIANO RONALDO DOS SANTOS AVEIRO
BORN: FEBRUARY 5, 1985
HEIGHT: 6'2"
TEAMS: SPORTING LISBON (PORTUGAL), MANCHESTER UNITED (ENGLAND), REAL MADRID (SPAIN)
INTERNATIONAL GAMES: 147
GOALS: 79

PORTUGAL

Ronaldo dashes across the field in a game against Hungary during the 2018 World Cup qualifications.

RONALDO

Despite the fact that his high self-esteem frustrates many, it is impossible to deny that Ronaldo is one of the most ambitious and powerful forwards in soccer history. And he is incredibly determined. After Messi had arrived on the world stage, it seemed like Ronaldo was condemned to live in his shadows, but through incessant training and ceaseless willpower, Ronaldo has managed to overtake Messi with regard both goals and awards. Ronaldo will be 33 years old when he travels to Russia, but no one should underestimate him. He could well carry Portugal far, like he did at the 2014 World Cup.

MEXICO

Javier Hernández, or Chicharito, will turn 23 years old just before the 2018 World Cup launches. Hailing from Guadalajara in Mexico, this bold player always comes across as a true lover of the game, bursting with youthful enthusiasm. Hernández has played in over 100 international games for Mexico, scoring on average a goal in every second game—goals of every possible variety, which is no wonder, given the fact that Hernandez is natural-born striker. Mexico has no shortage of veteran goal-scorers, for example Oribe, Peralta, and Carlos Vela. Since 1990, the soccer-crazed nation usually sprints effortlessly into the round of 16, but there the Mexicans always face some kind of impasse, leading to elimination. This time, they are determined to battle to the very end!

Javier Hernandez became Mexico's all-time top goalscorer, with his 47th, in a 2017 exhibition match against Croatia.

COSTA RICA

The Costa Ricans were a major hit at the 2014 World Cup, with their joyful, bold, and dynamic team, and their spirit carried them all the way to the quarterfinals. Costa Rica will make every effort to reignite their former spark in the arduous landscape that awaits them in Russia. The ever-agile Keylor Navas is their goalkeeping sentinel, and he is one of the best—Spanish giants Real Madrid choose him as their goalpost guardian!

PANAMA

A national celebration was held in Panama when the national team ensured a place in the final tournament of the World Cup for the first time. Panama's top goal-scorers Luis Tejada and Blas Pérez are now both in their late thirties, but the 2018 tournament whistle will definitely kick-off a newfound spirit of youth, regardless of age!

DENMARK 🇩🇰

The Danes are known for their light-hearted style but are often unpredictable. You could say that Danish fans are even more famous than the team itself, for their exuberant joy, loyalty and spirited encouragement. The most famous Dane this time around is Christian Eriksen, a brilliant midfielder, who has played a major role in Tottenham's recent triumphs.

SWEDEN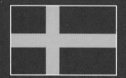

The Nordic countries have always played great soccer, and three of them—Sweden, Denmark, and Iceland—will join the final tournament in Russia. Sweden has the most successful World Cup heritage, twice reaching third place and once landing second. The Swedish team is more solid than spectacular, relying on a sturdy defense vigorously captained by Andreas Granqvist, and might face some challenges when it comes to goalscoring.

WILL ZLATAN JOIN THE PARTY?

The biggest question regarding Sweden's participation in 2018 revolves around the goalscoring legend Zlatan Ibrahimovic. Will he be temped to come out of retirement and grace the field one last time at the World Cup? Zlatan is 37 years old, but will enthrall true soccer fans in any arena.

Zlatan Ibrahimović

Christian Eriksen during the UEFA Champions League game between Tottenham Hotspur and Real Madrid .

ICELAND

One of the most spellbinding Cinderella stories of the World Cup concerns the subarctic island of Iceland. A nation with only 330,000 inhabitants succeeded in conquering the most challenging group of the World Cup qualifications, ensuring a seat in the Russian tournament. The national team has no world-class players in its ranks, aside from perhaps Gylfi Sigurðsson, who plays for Everton in England, but the team spirit is strong and the fighting spirit even stronger. The team coach is a dentist from a tiny fishing village, but don't be fooled by appearances— Icelanders have already proven that it's dangerous to underestimate them. And the country's achievements are not just down to luck. The team made it all the way to quarterfinals of the 2016 European Championship. No minor challenge awaits the Icelandic team in their very first game in Russia, where they will come face-to-face with the 2014 World Cup runners-up, Argentina, led by Lionel Messi.

Fans in the stands during the European Champanionship, Portugal vs Iceland, June 2016.

SOUTH KOREA

The Asian nations that enter the World Cup this year have few known international players in their ranks, aside from the South Korean Son Heung-min. His home country is counting on him to wear the national colors with the same cunning, intelligence, and goalscoring hunger that he has shown for the English team Tottenham.

Son Heung-min during the UEFA Champions League.

CROATIA

Croatia is a small European country in the Balkans with a population of only four million. The country has a rich soccer tradition, with a number of world-famous players, and a series of admirable achievements, both at the Euro and the World Cup (third place in 1998). This time, the Croatians present a powerful team in which the midfield maestro Luka Modric pulls all the strings. Modric is a modest genius who has tirelessly conducted the midfield for Real Madrid in recent years. With razor-sharp passes and positional intelligence, Modric has the ability to change the structure of the play in a single stroke. Other strong and gifted players such as Ivan Rakitić (Barcelona), Mario Mandžukić (Juventus), and Ivan Perišić (Inter Milan) shape Croatia into a force not to be reckoned with against any opponent.

WORLD CUP HISTORY
ALL THE TOURNAMENTS

Brazilian forwards Vava and Pele (number 10) enter a melee in front of the French goal during the the World Cup semi-final at the Rasunda Stadion in Solna, Stockholm, June 24, 1958. Brazil beat France 5-2.

URUGUAY | 1930

Only a handful of European nations could be bothered to set sail for Uruguay to participate in the first ever World Cup tournament. The powerful and skillful home team won a well-deserved victory. Uruguay had also won the gold at both the 1924 and 1928 Olympic Games.

WORLD CUP FINAL, JULY 30, 1930
ESTADIO CENTENARIO, MONTEVIDEO, URUGUAY

URUGUAY – ARGENTINA
4–2

DORADO 12	PEUCELLE 20
CEA 57	STÁBILE 37
IRIARTE 68	
CASTRO 89	

Estadio Centenario, Montevideo, Uruguay.

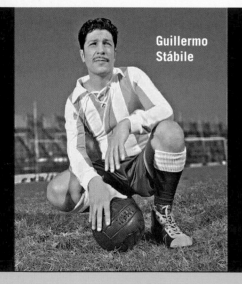

Guillermo Stábile

GOLD	**URUGUAY**
SILVER	ARGENTINA
BRONZE	USA
4TH PLACE	YUGOSLAVIA

BEST PLAYER: JOSÉ NASAZZI, URUGUAY

TOP GOALSCORER: GUILLERMO STÁBILE, ARGENTINA, 8 GOALS

NATIONS: 13

The game strategy in 1930 was very different from what we're used to nowadays. The most common setup now is placing four players in defense, four players in midfield and two in the offense. Back then, only two players manned the defense, three played midfield, and five handled the offense!

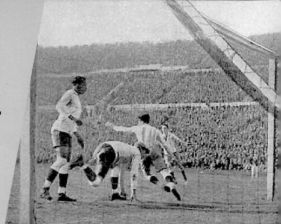

ITALY | 1934

The first qualification rounds were necessary for this World Cup, because 36 nations had applied to participate. There were no group stages at that time, so the 16 teams that had made it through the qualifications went straight to the knockout phase. Half of these nations were therefore eliminated after only one game, for example Brazil, who had traveled halfway across the globe, full of high hopes. An African nation participated for the first time: Egypt, who lost to Hungary during the qualification. Italy defeated the strong Slovakian and Czech team (which was then part of the same nation) in a final that went into extra time.

1934 top goal scorer
Oldřich Nejedlý.

WORLD CUP FINAL, JUNE 10, 1934
STADIO NATIONALE PNF, ROME, ITALY.

ITALY – CZECHOSLOVAKIA
2–1

ORSI 81   **PUČ 71**
SCHIAVIO 95

GOLD   **ITALY**
SILVER   CZECHOSLOVAKIA
BRONZE   GERMANY
4TH PLACE   AUSTRIA

BEST PLAYER: GIUSEPPE MEAZZA, ITALY

TOP GOALSCORER: OLDŘICH NEJEDLÝ, CZECHOSLOVAKIA, 5 GOALS

NATIONS: 16

Uruguay was offended by the lack of interest in the first World Cup, and refused to take part in the 1934 tournament. This is the first and only time that a reigning World Cup holder has decided not to defend the title.

FRANCE 1938

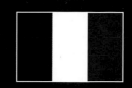

Once again, the tournament consisted only of the knockout phase. Brazil, led by the genius Leônidas, seemed to have the most promising team. During the semifinal, the Brazilian team was relaxed enough to put Leônidas on the bench in a game against the world champions themselves, and lost the game as a result. Italy therefore played in the final and managed to defend their title. This was the first of only two times that a team has succeeded in winning two tournaments in a row.

WORLD CUP FINAL, JUNE 19, 1938
STADE OLYMPIQUE DE COLOMBES, PARIS, FRANCE

ITALY – HUNGARY
4–2

COLAUSSI 6, 35	**TITKOS 8**
PIOLA 16, 82	**SÁROSI 70**
COLAUSSI 35	
PIOLA 82	

Leônidas da Silva is often credited with inventing the bicycle kick.

GOLD	**ITALY**
SILVER	HUNGARY
BRONZE	BRAZIL
4TH PLACE	SWEDEN

BEST PLAYER: LEÔNIDAS, BRAZIL

TOP GOALSCORER: LEÔNIDAS DA SILVA, BRAZIL, 7 GOALS

NATIONS: 15

The first team from Asia participated in the tournament—the then-titled Dutch East Indies, now Indonesia, which was an occupied colony of the Netherlands. The Dutch East Indies lost 6–0 to Hungary in their only game of the qualifications.

BRAZIL | 1950

Everyone believed that the Brazilian team would win the tournament, including the Brazilians themselves. They had a great offense-driven team which crushed one opponent after the other. Players such as Ademir, Chico, and Zizinho racked up goals, and were on top form. In the last game against Uruguay, a tie would be enough to secure the title. During that time, the tournament format was divided into two rounds, with no formal final. Around 200,000 eager spectators gathered in the Maracanã stadium to observe the glorious Brazilian victory. However, the powerhouse failed to deliver. The Brazilian team scored at the beginning of the second half, but the Uruguayans equalized, and then another goal which cast them in the lead, and definitively secured them their second World Cup. This came as a tremendous shock to Brazil.

WORLD CUP FINAL, JULY 16, 1950
MARACANÃ, RIO DE JANEIRO, BRAZIL

URUGUAY – BRAZIL
2–1

SCHIAFFINO 66   FRIAÇA 47
GHIGGIA 79

GOLD   **URUGUAY**
SILVER   BRAZIL
BRONZE   SWEDEN
4TH PLACE   SPAIN

BEST PLAYER: ADEMIR, BRAZIL

TOP GOALSCORER: ADEMIR, BRAZIL, 8 GOALS

NATIONS: 13

Ademir

England took part for the first time but, up until then the nation had been skeptical about the merits of the tournament. The team was eliminated following a 0–1 defeat at the hands of the US, considered then and now to be one of the most surprising results of a World Cup game.

SWITZERLAND ▮ 1954

This World Cup had a highly unexpected result. Hungary had boasted a near-invincible team, led by Puskás, Kocsis, and Hidegkuti. The Hungarian team was already at a 2–0 lead only eight minutes into the game, and they were expected to enjoy an easy victory. But West Germany, who had just begun to rise from the ashes of the Second World War, which had ended nine years earlier, leveled the game less than ten minutes later. This created enough momentum to carry the team to victory, and they scored the winning goals just moments before the game came to a close. The Germans dubbed the event "The Miracle of Bern." There are theories that the German players were injected with stimulants during halftime, which gave them the boost and endurance needed to overpower the sturdy Hungarian team, but these theories are unproven.

WORLD CUP FINAL, JULY 4, 1954
WANKDORF STADIUM, BERN, SWITZERLAND

WEST GERMANY – HUNGARY
3–2

MORLOCK 10	PUSKÁS 6
RAHN 18, 84	CZIBOR 8

Sándor Kocsis

GOLD   **WEST GERMANY**
SILVER   HUNGARY
BRONZE   AUSTRIA
4TH PLACE   URUGUAY

BEST PLAYER: FERENC PUSKÁS, HUNGARY

TOP GOALSCORER: SÁNDOR KOCSIS, HUNGARY, 11 GOALS

NATIONS: 16

The 1954 tournament saw a great number of goals. The Switzerland–Austria game holds the World Cup record for most goals in a single game. The Swiss team arrived at a 3–0 lead after 19 minutes but eventually lost the game 5–7!

SWEDEN | 1958

Brazil finally managed to clinch their long-awaited World Cup title, not least due to the performance of the 17-year-old genius Pelé. The Frenchman Fontaine set a new goalscoring record with a whopping 13 goals in six games.

GOLD   **BRAZIL**
SILVER   SWEDEN
BRONZE   FRANCE
4TH PLACE   WEST GERMANY

BEST PLAYER: DIDI, BRAZIL

TOP GOALSCORER: JUST FONTAINE, FRANCE, 13 GOALS

NATIONS: 16

WORLD CUP FINAL, JUNE 29, 1958
RÅSUNDA STADIUM, STOCKHOLM, SWEDEN

BRAZIL – SWEDEN
5–2

VAVÁ 9, 32	LIEDHOLM 4
PELÉ 55, 90	SIMONSSON 80
ZAGALLO 68	

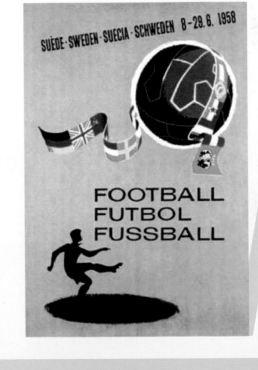

What was particularly noteworthy during the qualifications was in the "British Pot" of four seeded countries, Wales and Northern Ireland made it to the finals, whereas the larger soccer nations, England and Scotland, were eliminated.

The Brazilian forwards Vavá and Pelé (10) attack the Swedish goal during the World Cup Final.

43

CHILE | 1962

Brazil defended their World Cup title by defeating Sweden, and Chile landed their second silver. Pelé suffered an injury early in the tournament and the ever-nimble Garrincha dazzled the audience in his stead, but overall, Chile 1962 was considered a little dull.

WORLD CUP FINAL, JUNE 17, 1962
ESTADIO NACIONAL, NUNOA,
SANTIAGO, CHILE

BRAZIL – CZECHOSLOVAKIA
3–1

AMARILDO 17	MASOPUST 15
ZITO 69	
VAVÁ 78	

CAMPEONATO MUNDIAL DE FUTBOL
WORLD FOOTBALL CHAMPIONSHIP
CHAMPIONNAT MONDIAL DE FOOTBALL
COUPE JULES RIMET

CHILE 1962

Garrincha during the 1962 World Cup. Garrincha is a nickname, meaning "little bird."

GOLD **BRAZIL**
SILVER CZECHOSLOVAKIA
BRONZE CHILE
4TH PLACE YUGOSLAVIA

BEST PLAYERS: GARRINCHA, BRAZIL

TOP GOAL-SCORERS: GARRINCHA, BRAZIL
VAVÁ, BRAZIL; LEONEL SÁNCHEZ, CHILE;
FLÓRÍAN ALBERT, HUNGARY;
VALENTIN IVANOV, SOVIET UNION;
DRAŽAN JERKOVIĆ, YUGOSLAVIA;
4 GOALS EACH

NATIONS: 16

Vavá became the first player to score in two World Cup finals.

ENGLAND ▮ 1966

England won their only major tournament title on home territory. The tournament was characterized by tough and even tedious soccer, though Eusébio's skillful maneuvers were a delight to watch. The completely unknown North Korean team attracted attention by defeating two-time champions Italy 1–0, thereby entering the quarterfinals.

WORLD CUP FINAL, JULY 30, 1966
WEMBLEY STADIUM, LONDON, ENGLAND

ENGLAND – WEST GERMANY
4–2

HURST 18, 101, 120	**HALLER 12**
PETERS 78	**WEBER 89**

GOLD — **ENGLAND**
SILVER — WEST GERMANY
BRONZE — PORTUGAL
4TH PLACE — SOVIET UNION

BEST PLAYER: BOBBY CHARLTON, ENGLAND

TOP GOALSCORER: EUSÉBIO, PORTUGAL, 9 GOALS

NATIONS: 16

Geoff Hurst is the only player to have scored a hat trick in a World Cup Final. Even today, there is still some debate over the validity of his second goal, and whether or not it crossed the line.

Eusébio during a game against Hungary at the 1966 World Cup.

MEXICO | 1970

This was a fantastic tournament in which the brilliant Brazilian team won an amazing victory in a thrilling final. The dazzling teamplay of the Brazilians was unstoppable. They won all of their games, both in the South American qualifications and during the final tournament in Mexico. After this, no one could doubt that Pelé was the world's greatest soccer player, and Brazil became the first country to win three World Cup titles.

WORLD CUP FINAL, JUNE 21, 1970
ESTADIO AZTECA, MEXICO CITY, MEXICO

BRAZIL – ITALY
4–1

PELÉ 18	BONINSEGNA 37
GÉRSON 66	
JAIRZINHO 71	
CARLOS ALBERTO 86	

Pelé makes a shot during a game against Czechoslovakia.

GOLD **BRAZIL**
SILVER ITALY
BRONZE WEST GERMANY
4TH PLACE URUGUAY

BEST PLAYER: PELÉ, BRAZIL

TOP GOALSCORER: GERD MÜLLER, WEST GERMANY, 10 GOALS.

NATIONS: 16

The Brazilian Jairzinho managed the Herculean task of scoring a goal in every game during the final tournament. He scored a total of seven goals in six games.

PELÉ

THE GREATEST EVER

BRAZIL

Pelé had become a national hero in 1958. He was awarded the title "official national "treasure," and was prohibited from playing for foreign teams until the end of his career. He was the symbol for everything that was great about Brazilian soccer —tremendously agile and cunning, relentless attacking spirit, powerful shot—yes, he excels in almost every aspect of the game, and apparently he is a great goalkeeper to boot!

During the 1958 World Cup in Sweden, he was given the number 10 jersey by sheer coincidence. Since then, the position Pelé played on the field has come to be referred to as the "10." This means that he played just behind the strikers, directed the offense, but also broke through the opponent's defense and racked up countless goals. Pelé took home three cups with Brazil, and doubtlessly could have joined the ranks of the Brazilian team in 1974, but by that time he had left the national team. Many consider Pelé the greatest soccer player of all time, yet supporters of Maradona and Messi are quick to dispute this claim!

FULL NAME:
EDSON ARANTES DO NASCIMENTO
BORN: OCTOBER 3, 1940
HEIGHT: 5'8"
TEAMS: SANTOS (BRAZIL), NEW YORK COSMOS (USA)
INTERNATIONAL GAMES: 1957–1971, 92
GOALS: 77

WEST GERMANY  1974

The Brazilian team seemed utterly lost without their Pelé. And a new powerhouse had entered the scene: Holland played magnificently and no one surpassed the immensely gifted Johan Cruyff. Many hoped that Cruyff's incredible agility would inevitably land the "total soccer" Dutch team their title. However, the highly organized home team, led by Franz "The Emperor" Beckenbauer, managed to quell the Dutch upsurge.

Gerd Müller celebrates the World Cup title after having scored the winning goal against Holland.

WORLD CUP FINAL, JULY 7, 1974
OLYMPIASTADION, MUNICH

WEST GERMANY – HOLLAND
2–1

BREITNER (PENALTY) 25   NEESKENS (PENALTY) 2
G. MÜLLER 43

GOLD	**WEST GERMANY**
SILVER	HOLLAND
BRONZE	POLAND
4TH PLACE	BRAZIL

BEST PLAYER: JOHAN CRUYFF, HOLLAND

TOP GOALSCORER: GRZEGORZ LATO, POLAND, 7 GOALS

NATIONS: 16

The German striker Gerd Müller or "Der Bomber" (top goalscorer in 1970) scored four goals in the tournament, amassing a total of 14 goals in World Cup finals, and snatching the record from Fontaine. To be fair, Fontaine had scored all his goals during a single tournament!

ARGENTINA | 1978

The Dutch team played without Cruyff, and lost to the fierce Argentine team in a game that extended into extra time. A gloomy atmosphere presided over the tournament, which was understandable, given the fact that it was hosted by a military dictatorship that had taken power through a coup.

Kempes was the top goalscorer of the tournament, scoring two goals in the final against Holland.

WORLD CUP FINAL, JUNE 25, 1978
ESTADIO MONUMENTAL, BUENOS AIRES, ARGENTINA

ARGENTINA – HOLLAND
3–1

KEMPES 37, 104   NANNINGA 82
BERTONI 115

GOLD	ARGENTINA
SILVER	HOLLAND
BRONZE	BRAZIL
4TH PLACE	ITALY

BEST PLAYER: MARIO KEMPES, ARGENTINA

TOP GOALSCORER: MARIO KEMPES, ARGENTINA, 6 GOALS.

NATIONS: 16

Argentina 78

Brazil was eliminated before it could reach the final, even though the team was victorious in every game they played. This was due to the special format of the tournament, which was designed to suit the needs of the home team. Brazil is therefore the only team that has made it undefeated through a World Cup tournament, but nevertheless were not awarded the gold.

SPAIN | 1982

The tournament was not without controversy. Algeria was close to becoming the first African nation to qualify to the second round, but the Germans and Austrians seemed like they had already agreed on the result of their game, which essentially prevented Algeria from progressing. This was a pure disgrace. On the other hand, the magnificent play of the Brazilian team was a beautiful sight. Brazil exhibited great teamwork, echoing the days of Pelé, this time with Zico and Sócrates in the forefront. The second round saw life return to the sluggish Italian team as they returned to form, and managed to eliminate Brazil.

Germany faced France in a historic 3–3 game, though the Germans secured victory in the penalty shootout. At the height of the game, the German goalkeeper Schumacher wildly collided with the Frenchman Battiston, who lost two teeth, and suffered three broken ribs. Schumacher's behavior was considered symbolic of the German strategy, which at that time was more about aggression than skill. The exhausted Germans proved little hindrance to the Italian team, leading to Italy securing their third World Cup.

ESPAÑA 82

WORLD CUP FINAL, JULY 11, 1982
SANTIAGO BERNABÉU, MADRID, SPAIN

ITALY – WEST GERMANY
3–1

ROSSI 57	BREITNER 83
TARDELLI 69	
ALTOBELLI 81	

GOLD   **ITALY**
SILVER   WEST GERMANY
BRONZE   POLAND
4TH PLACE   FRANCE

BEST PLAYER: PAOLO ROSSI, ITALY
TOP GOALSCORER: PAOLO ROSSI, ITALY, 6 GOALS

NATIONS: 16

It was through sheer luck that Italy made it out of the first group stage. Both Italy and Cameroon had made three draws in their group, but Italy's total score exceeded Cameroon's by only one goal, landing Italy in second place, which was just enough to open the door to the next round.

MEXICO | 1986

At this World Cup, the number of teams increased to 24. Morocco became the first African nation to win the group stages, and enter the knockout stage. There, the Moroccan team lost 0-1 to Germany. Brazil's performance was no less spectacular than in 1982, but they were eventually defeated by France during a penalty shootout in the quarterfinals. France, led by Platini, then lost to the well-oiled German machine. The Germans met the Argentine team in the final, where the legendary Maradona was involved in every aspect of the game. Maradona almost single-handedly carried the otherwise mediocre Argentina to the final. In a famous game against England during the quarterfinals, Maradona first scored with "the Hand of God," which he then followed up with one of the most glorious goals of any World Cup tournament. Maradona then led his men to victory and Argentina was awarded its second World Cup.

WORLD CUP FINAL, JUNE 29, 1982
ESTADIO AZTECA, MEXICO CITY, MEXICO

ARGENTINA – WEST GERMANY
3–2

BROWN 23	**RUMMENIGGE 74**
VALDANO 55	**VÖLLER 80**
BURRUCHAGA 83	

GOLD   **ARGENTINA**
SILVER   WEST GERMANY
BRONZE   FRANCE
4TH PLACE   BELGIUM

BEST PLAYER: DIEGO MARADONA, ARGENTINA

TOP GOALSCORER: GARY LINEKER, ENGLAND, 6 GOALS.

NATIONS: 24

Denmark qualified for the World Cup for the fist time. The red and white "Danish Dynamite" attracted attention for a joyous and spirited style.

THE LEGEND
MARADONA

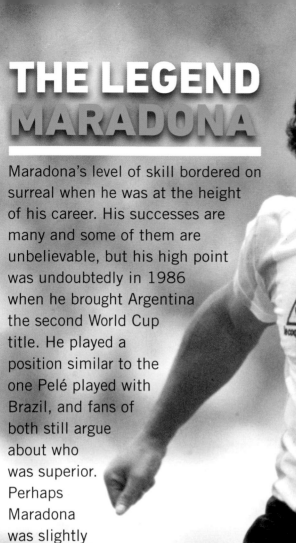

Maradona's level of skill bordered on surreal when he was at the height of his career. His successes are many and some of them are unbelievable, but his high point was undoubtedly in 1986 when he brought Argentina the second World Cup title. He played a position similar to the one Pelé played with Brazil, and fans of both still argue about who was superior. Perhaps Maradona was slightly more agile but he was not as determined and precise as Pelé in terms of goalscoring. Maradona's private life was unfortunately turbulent. He struggled with drug addiction, resulting in expulsion from the 1994 World Cup. He thankfully recovered, to the extent that he was able to serve as head coach of the Argentine national team. Maradona approaches every task with passion and commitment, and this was no exception.

Maradona in full throttle during the 1986 World Cup.

NAME: DIEGO ARMANDO MARADONA
BORN: OCTOBER 30, 1960
HEIGHT: 5'5"
TEAMS: BOCA JUNIORS (ARGENTINA), BARCELONA, SEVILLA (BOTH SPAIN), NAPOLI (ITALY)
INTERNATIONAL GAMES: 1977–1994, 91
GOALS: 34

ITALY | 1990

This was perhaps the most tedious World Cup tournament in history. Most teams played in a lifeless and defense-orientated style, with the only thing to please soccer fans being Cameroon's performance. The team conquered Argentina 1–0 in the first game. In the next game, the 38-year-old Roger Milla, who returned from retirement to join the national team, scored the two goals of a 2–1 victory over Romania. During the round of 16, Cameroon beat Colombia, but was eventually defeated by England 2–3, in a game that went into extra time. An ankle injury plagued Maradona but still he led the Argentine team through two penalty shootouts, and then to the final, which was considered one of the dullest in recent memory.

WORLD CUP FINAL, JUNE 8, 1990
STADIO OLIMPICO, ROME, ITALY

WEST GERMANY – ARGENTINA
1–0

BREHME 85
(PENALTY)

GOLD   **WEST GERMANY**
SILVER   ARGENTINA
BRONZE   ITALY
4TH PLACE   ENGLAND

TOP GOALSCORER AND BEST PLAYER: SALVATORE SCHILLACI, ITALY, 6 GOALS.

NATIONS: 24

West Germany played their third final in a row, and were finally victorious.

Roger Milla celebrates after a goal against Colombia.

USA I 1994

Saud Arabia qualified for the World Cup for the first time. During the knockout phase, the Saudis lost to the Swedish team, whose lively style came as a surprise to many. The powerful Nigerian team made it to the round of 16 after great success in the group stages, but ultimately lost to the Italians. Brazil finally took home their fourth World Cup title, but despite top performances from Romário and Bebeto, the team was far from playing its characteristic skillful and dynamic soccer. The results of the dull final were resolved by a penalty shootout for the first time. Italy's leading player, Roberto Baggio, missed the team's last shot.

WORLD CUP FINAL, JULY 17, 1994
ROSE BOWL, PASADENA, CALIFORNIA, USA

BRAZIL – ITALY
0–0 (3–2 PENALTY SHOOTOUT)

GOLD	**BRAZIL**
SILVER	ITALY
BRONZE	SWEDEN
4TH PLACE	BULGARIA

BEST PLAYER: ROMÁRIO, BRAZIL

TOP GOALSCORERS: OLEG SALENKO, RUSSIA, HRISTO STOICHKOV, BULGARIA, 6 GOALS EACH

NATIONS: 24

Romário de Souza Faria

Romário's first goal in the 1994 World Cup Final arrived in the penalty shootout. The Brazilian forward was no slouch when it came to scoring goals. He scored a total of 734 goals in his career, including 55 goals in 70 international games.

FRANCE | 1998

The young Brazilian genius Ronaldo was in top form throughout most of the tournament, but when his team appeared in the final he suddenly lost all of his spark and flair. It came to light that Ronaldo had suffered a seizure the previous night, and should not have played in the match. Brazil was consequently an easy prey to the animated French team, captained by the French legend Zidane.

WORLD CUP FINAL, JULY 12, 1998
STADE DE FRANCE, PARIS, FRANCE

FRANCE – BRAZIL
3–0

ZIDANE 27, 46+
PETIT 93+

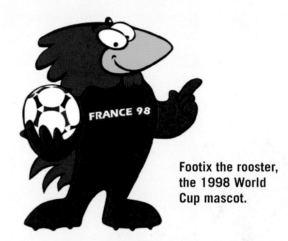

Footix the rooster, the 1998 World Cup mascot.

Zidane made two goals in the final against Brazil.

GOLD	FRANCE
SILVER	BRAZIL
BRONZE	CROATIA
4TH PLACE	HOLLAND

BEST PLAYER: RONALDO, BRAZIL

TOP GOALSCORER: DAVOR ŠUKER, CROATIA, 6 GOALS

NATIONS: 32

Norway qualified for the tournament for the first time, and defeated Brazil in the group stages, but then lost to Italy in the round of 16.

JAPAN AND SOUTH KOREA | 2002

This was a World Cup of firsts—two nations hosting the tournament, the World Cup taking place in Asia, and an Asian team (South Korea) reaching the semifinals (albeit aided by a series of refereeing scandals, especially against Italy). No less surprising was the fact that Turkey secured a spot in the semifinals. However, the powerhouses Brazil and Germany were not intimidated by a couple of surprises, and breezed into the final. The Germans placed their faith in a tight-knit defense strategy, with a strong goalkeeper (Oliver Kahn), whereas Brazil relied on the brilliance of Ronaldo, who was firing on all cylinders again. No less impressive were the performances of legends Rivaldo and Ronaldinho.

WORLD CUP FINAL, JUNE 30, 2002
YOKOHAMA INTERNATIONAL, YOKOHAMA, JAPAN

BRAZIL – GERMANY
2–0

RONALDO 67, 79

GOLD	**BRAZIL**
SILVER	GERMANY
BRONZE	TURKEY
4TH PLACE	SOUTH KOREA

BEST PLAYER:
OLIVER KAHN, GERMANY

TOP GOALSCORER:
RONALDO, BRAZIL, 8 GOALS.

NATIONS: 32

The Brazilian defender Cafu set a record when he played his third consecutive World Cup final. He had played for part of the game in 1994, but in 1998 and 2002 he was on the field from start to finish. Despite the fact that West Germany had played three consecutive finals, 1982–1990, none of Germany's players participated in all three games.

Ronaldo and Rivaldo celebrate the 2002 World Cup title.

GERMANY | 2006

This tournament will be forever marked by Zidane's infamous head-butt of the Italian Materazzi in the 110th minute during extra time. Zidane had been considered one of the world's greatest soccer players. Both Zidane and Materazzi had scored before the game went into extra time. The Italian was a wily defender, and reputedly he made a few insulting remarks about Zidane's sister, in order to rile Zidane up.

It worked, and Zidane received the red card and was sent off. Everyone scored in the penalty shootout apart from the Frenchman Trézéguet, and Italy won the title, to considerable astonishment. The biggest surprise in the tournament, however, was Germany's light and spirited style, given their reputation for toughness and ferocity.

WORLD CUP FINAL, JULY 9, 2006
OLYMPIASTADION, BERLIN, GERMANY

ITALY – FRANCE
1–1 (5–3 IN PENALTY SHOOTOUT)

MATERAZZI 19   ZIDANE 7

Zidane head-butted Materazzi in the final.

FIFA WORLD CUP
GERMANY
2006

© 2002 FIFA TM

GOLD	**ITALY**
SILVER	FRANCE
BRONZE	GERMANY
4TH PLACE	PORTUGAL

BEST PLAYER:
ZINEDINE ZIDANE, FRANCE

TOP GOALSCORER: MIROSLAV KLOSE, GERMANY, 5 GOALS

32 NATIONS

Ronaldo's performance was subdued during the tournament, but he still scored three times. His goals then totaled 15—four in the 1998 World Cup, and eight in 2002—which was a record at that time.

SOUTH AFRICA | 2010

The first World Cup held in Africa was was less than inspiring. Spain, at that time a great team, brought home the World Cup. The final was disappointing and Holland played without their usual flair and fluidity. Eventually, the midfield genius Iniesta scored the winning goal in extra time.

WORLD CUP FINAL, JULY 11, 2010
SOCCER CITY, JOHANNESBURG, SOUTH AFRICA

SPAIN – HOLLAND
1–0
INIESTA 116

Two legends—Messi on the field, Maradona as coach—were not enough to make Argentina champions. Argentina suffered a humiliating 0–4 defeat at the hands of the Germans during the quarterfinals.

GOLD   **SPAIN**
SILVER   HOLLAND
BRONZE   GERMANY
4TH PLACE   URUGUAY

BEST PLAYER: DIEGO FORLÁN, URUGUAY

TOP GOALSCORERS: THOMAS MÜLLER, GERMANY; DIEGO FORLÁN, URUGUAY; WESLEY SCHNEIDER, HOLLAND; DAVID VILA, SPAIN; 6 GOALS EACH

NATIONS: 32

The twenty-first century saw Spain assemble a tremendous team in which the midfielders Xavi (8, right) and Iniesta (21, left) played the leading roles, winning three consecutive tournaments: the 2008 UEFA Euro, the 2010 World Cup, and the 2012 UEFA Euro.

BRAZIL | 2014

Germany played like a well-oiled machine and defeated Brazil 7–1 in the semifinals, to the unbelievable horror of the host country, who had intended to settle the "mistake" that had taken place on the same field in 1950. Brazil's biggest star, Neymar, suffered an injury in the quarterfinals against Colombia and was unable to play. Leo Messi managed to carry the rather lackluster Argentine team to the final, but he failed to find his form during the game. The substitute Mario Götze scored the winning goal toward the end of extra time. The tournament's biggest surprise was Costa Rica, who made it to the quarterfinals.

WORLD CUP FINAL, JULY 13, 2014
ESTÁDIO DO MARACANÃ, RIO DE JANEIRO, BRAZIL

GERMANY – ARGENTINA
1–0

GÖTZE 113

The Brazilians Dani Alves (left) and David Luiz (right) console James Rodriguez following Colombia's defeat against Brazil.

Götze lifts the cup.

GOLD	**GERMANY**
SILVER	ARGENTINA
BRONZE	HOLLAND
4TH PLACE	BRAZIL

BEST PLAYER: LEO MESSI, ARGENTINA

TOP GOALSCORER: JAMES RODRIGUEZ, COLOMBIA, 6 GOALS

NATIONS: 32

Klose scored two goals for Germany, and beat Ronaldo's goalscoring record. He scored 16 goals in four tournaments—five in both 2005 and 2006, and four in the 2010 World Cup.

GROUP STAGE
MATCH SCHEDULE

A

	SCORE	
JUNE 14, 11:00 AM **RUSSIA**		MOSCOW **SAUDI ARABIA**
JUNE 15, 8:00 AM **EGYPT**		YEKATERINBURG **URUGAY**
JUNE 19, 2:00 PM **RUSSIA**		ST. PETERSBURG **EGYPT**
JUNE 20, 11:00 AM **URUGAY**		ROSTOV-ON-DON **SAUDI ARABIA**
JUNE 25, 10:00 AM **URUGAY**		SAMARA **RUSSIA**
JUNE 25, 10:00 AM **SAUDI ARABIA**		VOLGOGRAD **EGYPT**

TEAM	P	W	D	L	F	A	PTS

B

	SCORE	
JUNE 15, 11:00 AM **MOROCCO**		ST. PETERSBURG **IRAN**
JUNE 15, 2:00 PM **PORTUGAL**		SOCHI **SPAIN**
JUNE 20, 8:00 AM **PORTUGAL**		MOSCOW **MOROCCO**
JUNE 20, 2:00 PM **IRAN**		KAZAN **SPAIN**
JUNE 25, 2:00 PM **IRAN**		SARANSK **PORTUGAL**
JUNE 25, 2:00 PM **SPAIN**		KALININGRAD **MOROCCO**

TEAM	P	W	D	L	F	A	PTS

C

	SCORE	
JUNE 16, 6:00 AM **FRANCE**		KAZAN **AUSTRALIA**
JUNE 16, 12:00 AM **PERU**		SARANSK **DENMARK**
JUNE 21, 8:00 AM **DENMARK**		SAMARA **AUSTRALIA**
JUNE 21, 11:00 AM **FRANCE**		YEKATERINBURG **PERU**
JUNE 26, 10:00 AM **DENMARK**		MOSCOW **FRANCE**
JUNE 26, 10:00 AM **AUSTRALIA**		SOCHI **PERU**

TEAM	P	W	D	L	F	A	PTS

D

	SCORE	
JUNE 16, 9:00 AM **ARGENTINA**		MOSCOW **ICELAND**
JUNE 16, 3:00 PM **CROATIA**		KALININGRAD **NIGERIA**
JUNE 21, 2:00 PM **ARGENTINA**		NIZHNY NOVGOROD **CROATIA**
JUNE 22, 11:00 AM **NIGERIA**		VOLGOGRAD **ICELAND**
JUNE 26, 2:00 PM **NIGERIA**		ST. PETERSBURG **ARGENTINA**
JUNE 26, 2:00 PM **ICELAND**		ROSTOV-ON-DON **CROATIA**

TEAM	P	W	D	L	F	A	PTS

ALL MATCHES ARE LISTED
IN EASTERN STANDARD TIME

GROUP STAGE KEY

P = played; W = win; D = draw; L = loss; F = goals for;
A = goals against; Pts = points.

Three points for a win; one for a draw; no points for a loss.
After points, rankings are determined by goal difference in all
group matches, then by number of goals scored in all group
matches. If two or more teams are still equal, the results
between these teams determine the rankings. (If teams are still
equal, then fair play conduct determines rank, then finally the
FIFA Organising Committee draws lots.)

E

Match	SCORE	Opponent
JUNE 17, 8:00 AM **COSTA RICA**		SAMARA **SERBIA**
JUNE 17, 2:00 PM **BRAZIL**		ROSTOV-ON-DON **SWITZERLAND**
JUNE 22, 8:00 AM **BRAZIL**		ST. PETERSBURG **COSTA RICA**
JUNE 22, 2:00 PM **SERBIA**		KALININGRAD **SWITZERLAND**
JUNE 27, 2:00 PM **SERBIA**		MOSCOW **BRAZIL**
JUNE 27, 2:00 PM **SWITZERLAND**		NIZHNY NOVGOROD **COSTA RICA**

TEAM	P	W	D	L	F	A	PTS

F

Match	SCORE	Opponent
JUNE 17, 11:00 AM **GERMANY**		MOSCOW **MEXICO**
JUNE 18, 8:00 AM **SWEDEN**		NIZHNY NOVGOROD **SOUTH KOREA**
JUNE 23, 11:00 AM **SOUTH KOREA**		ROSTOV-ON-DON **MEXICO**
JUNE 23, 2:00 PM **GERMANY**		SOCHI **SWEDEN**
JUNE 27, 10:00 AM **SOUTH KOREA**		KAZAN **GERMANY**
JUNE 27, 10:00 AM **MEXICO**		YEKATERINBURG **SWEDEN**

TEAM	P	W	D	L	F	A	PTS

G

Match	SCORE	Opponent
JUNE 18, 11:00 AM **BELGIUM**		SOCHI **PANAMA**
JUNE 18, 2:00 PM **TUNISIA**		VOLGOGRAD **ENGLAND**
JUNE 23, 8:00 AM **BELGIUM**		MOSCOW **TUNISIA**
JUNE 24, 8:00 AM **ENGLAND**		NIZHNY NOVGOROD **PANAMA**
JUNE 28, 2:00 PM **ENGLAND**		KALININGRAD **BELGIUM**
JUNE 28, 2:00 PM **PANAMA**		SARANSK **TUNISIA**

TEAM	P	W	D	L	F	A	PTS

H

Match	SCORE	Opponent
JUNE 19, 8:00 AM **COLOMBIA**		SARANSK **JAPAN**
JUNE 19, 11:00 AM **POLAND**		MOSCOW **SENEGAL**
JUNE 24, 11:00 PM **JAPAN**		YEKATERINBURG **SENEGAL**
JUNE 24, 2:00 PM **POLAND**		KAZAN **COLOMBIA**
JUNE 28, 10:00 AM **JAPAN**		VOLGOGRAD **POLAND**
JUNE 28, 10:00 AM **SENEGAL**		SAMARA **COLOMBIA**

TEAM	P	W	D	L	F	A	PTS

KNOCKOUT STAGE
MATCH SCHEDULE

ROUND OF 16

	SCORE	
JUNE 30, 10:00 AM **1C**		KAZAN **2D**
JUNE 30, 2:00 PM **1A**		SOCHI **2B**
JULY 1, 10:00 AM **1B**		MOSCOW **2A**
JULY 1, 2:00 PM **1D**		NIZHNY NOVGOROD **2C**
JULY 2, 10:00 AM **1E**		SAMARA **2F**
JULY 2, 2:00 PM **1G**		ROSTOV-ON-DON **2H**
JULY 3, 10:00 AM **1F**		ST. PETERSBURG **2E**
JULY 3, 2:00 PM **1H**		MOSCOW **2G**

Note: The alphanumeric designations in the Round of 16 refer to first-round group positions:
1A is the winner of Group A, 2C is the runner-up in Group C.

QUARTERFINALS

	SCORE	
JULY 6, 10:00 AM **W49**		NIZHNY NOVGOROD **W50**
JULY 6, 2:00 PM **W53**		KAZAN **W54**
JULY 7, 10:00 AM **W55**		SAMARA **W56**
JULY 7, 2:00 PM **W51**		SOCHI **W52**

ALL MATCHES ARE LISTED
IN EASTERN STANDARD TIME